Unicorns Activity Book

HELLO!

Welcome to the world of magical unicorns. We're here to guide you through this book of games and activities!

Let's have some fun!

English edition © 2024 Happy Fox Books,
an imprint of Fox Chapel Publishing Company, Inc., 903 Square Street, Mount Joy, PA 17552.

© 2021 Clorophyl Éditions – 2, Le Gué –35380 Plélan-Le-Grand – France

Editorial coordination: Idées Book | Graphic design: L'épicerie graphique | Illustrations: Shutterstock.com

ISBN: 978-1-64124-395-7
All rights reserved.
Printed in China
First Printing

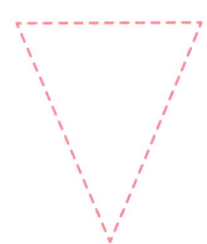
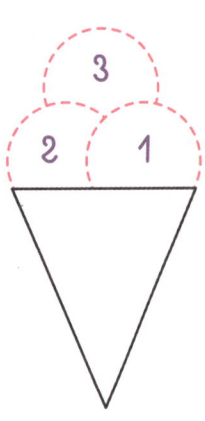
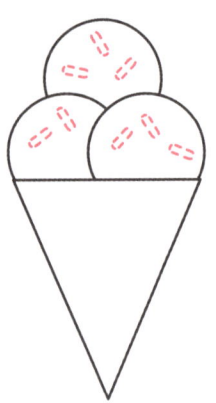

1. Draw an upside-down triangle for the cone.

2. Add three circles inside for the scoops.

3. Draw on sprinkles.

4. Color!

DRAW AN ICE-CREAM CONE
Learn to draw an ice-cream cone, color it, then fill the page with these delicious treats!

HAVE YOU SEEN GUMDROP?
Out of all the unicorns on the page,
find this one and circle her.

Choose the correct drawing.

1 2 3

SUDO-DRAWINGS
In order to have the cat, cake, and present shown in each row and in each column, which drawing is missing?

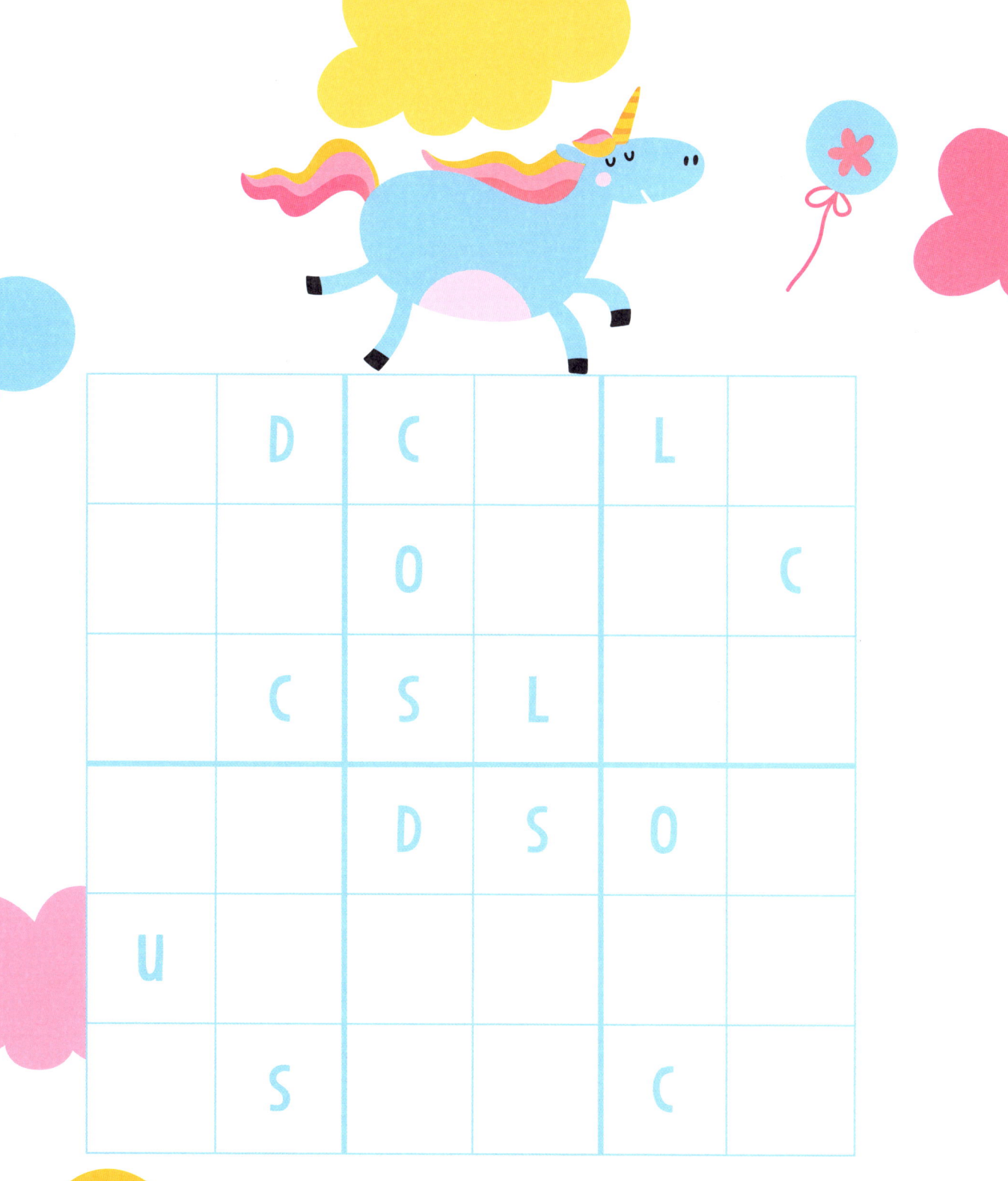

SUDO-WORD
Complete the grid so that the six letters
of the word CLOUDS are found on each line, in each column,
and in each group of six boxes.

 EXIT

 ENTER

PATTERN:

FOLLOW THE PATTERN

Help Lollipop find the exit by following the pattern of treats.
The pattern can move side to side or up and down.

PUZZLE
Cut out the puzzle pieces following the dotted lines, mix them up, and put the drawing back together as quickly as possible.

SPOT THE DIFFERENCES
Find and circle the seven differences between these two images.

HAVE YOU SEEN THIS GLASSES BADGE?

Help Rainbow find the glasses badge out of all the badges on the page. Circle it!

5					
	4	2	6	5	
	2	5	4	1	
	3	1	5	6	
		4		3	
1					6

SUDOKU
Complete the grid so that the numbers one to six are found on each line, in each column, and in each group of six boxes.

HOW FAST CAN YOU COUNT?
How many of these castles are there on the page? Write the answer in the bubble.

C	H	L	I	L	A	C	P
E	T	L	Y	R	O	S	E
L	U	I	J	S	I	V	T
O	L	L	R	O	E	S	U
T	I	Y	R	F	N	E	N
U	P	D	M	U	M	C	I
S	D	A	I	S	Y	E	A

LILAC – MUM – IRIS – TULIP
ROSE – PETUNIA – LILY
DAISY – LOTUS

WORD SEARCH
Circle the names of flowers in the grid.
They can be written side to side,
up and down, or diagonally.

13

SUDO-SHAPES

Complete the grid so that all six shapes are found on each line, in each column, and in each group of six boxes.

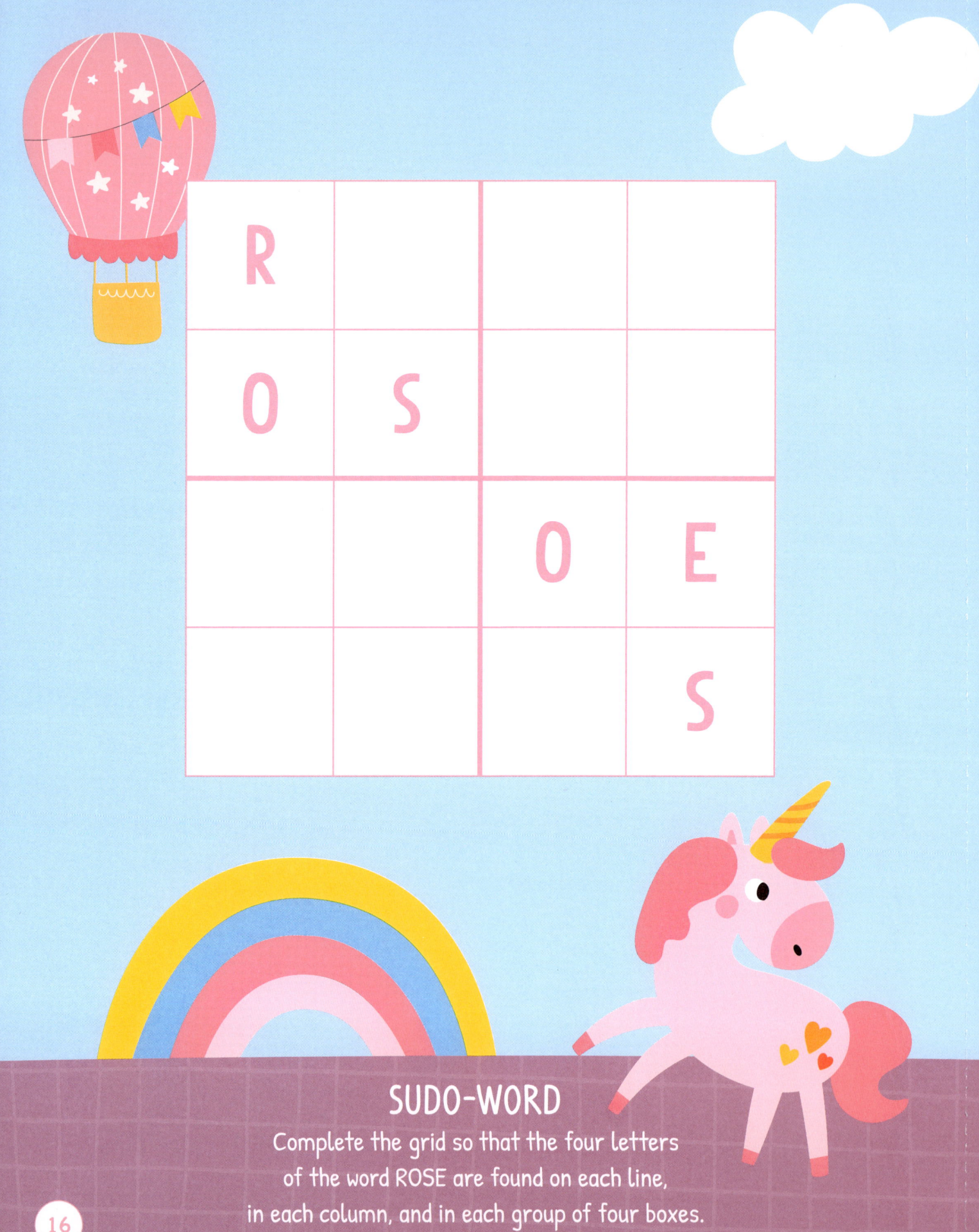

SUDO-WORD
Complete the grid so that the four letters of the word ROSE are found on each line, in each column, and in each group of four boxes.

WHERE IS MY SHADOW?
Match each unicorn to their shadow.

SUDO-COLORS

Color the flowers yellow, green, pink, or blue.
Each color must appear only once on each line, in each column,
and in each square of four boxes.

FOLLOW THE PATTERN
Help Shimmer find the exit by following the pattern of pictures.
The pattern can move side to side or up and down.

SEEK AND FIND
Look throughout the nighttime scene to find and circle these drawings within!

PUZZLE

Match the last three pieces to complete the puzzle!
Put the correct number in each blank triangle.

COMPLETE THE PATTERN
Complete the pattern by coloring in the crowns and following the arrows!

Pattern:

Choose the correct drawing.

1   2   3

SUDO-DRAWINGS
In order to have the striped, pink, and blue envelope shown in each row and in each column, which drawing is missing?

PORTRAIT
Only one of these portraits of Candy the caticorn is correct.
Which one is it?

ODD ONE OUT

Another animal has slipped in among the unicorns. Out of all the animals on this page, find and circle the odd one out.

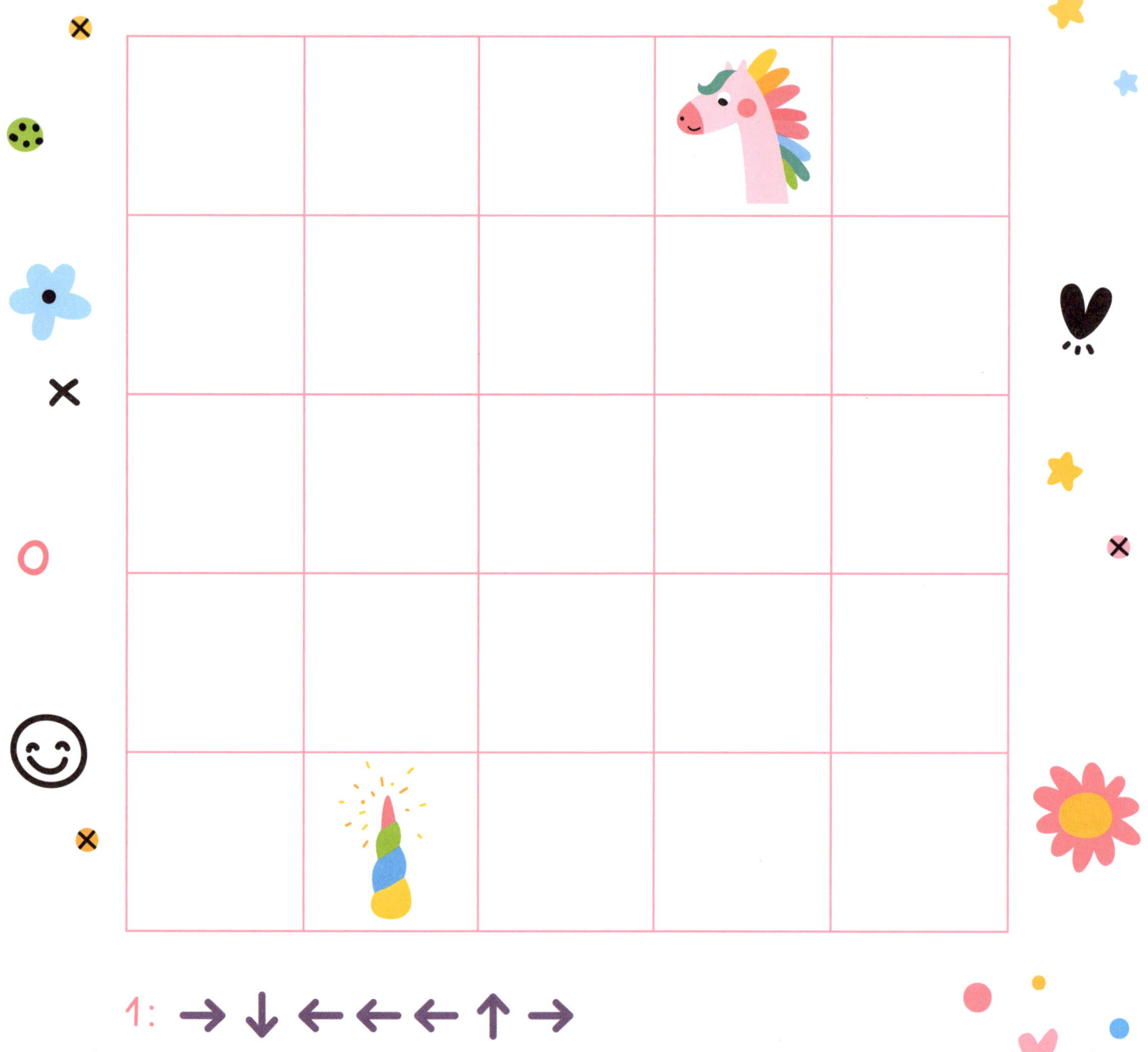

1: → ↓ ← ← ← ↑ →
2: ← ← ← ↓ → →
3: ↓ ← ↓ ← ← ↓ ↓ →

CODING

Shimmer needs to find her horn, but she doesn't know the correct code! Which of these three codes is the correct one if you start in the box with the unicorn?

COMPLETE THE PATTERN
Complete the pattern by coloring in the hearts and following the arrows!

WHERE IS MY SHADOW?
Which shadow belongs to Sylvie the swanicorn?

PORTRAIT
Only one of these portraits of Pinky is correct.
Which one is it?

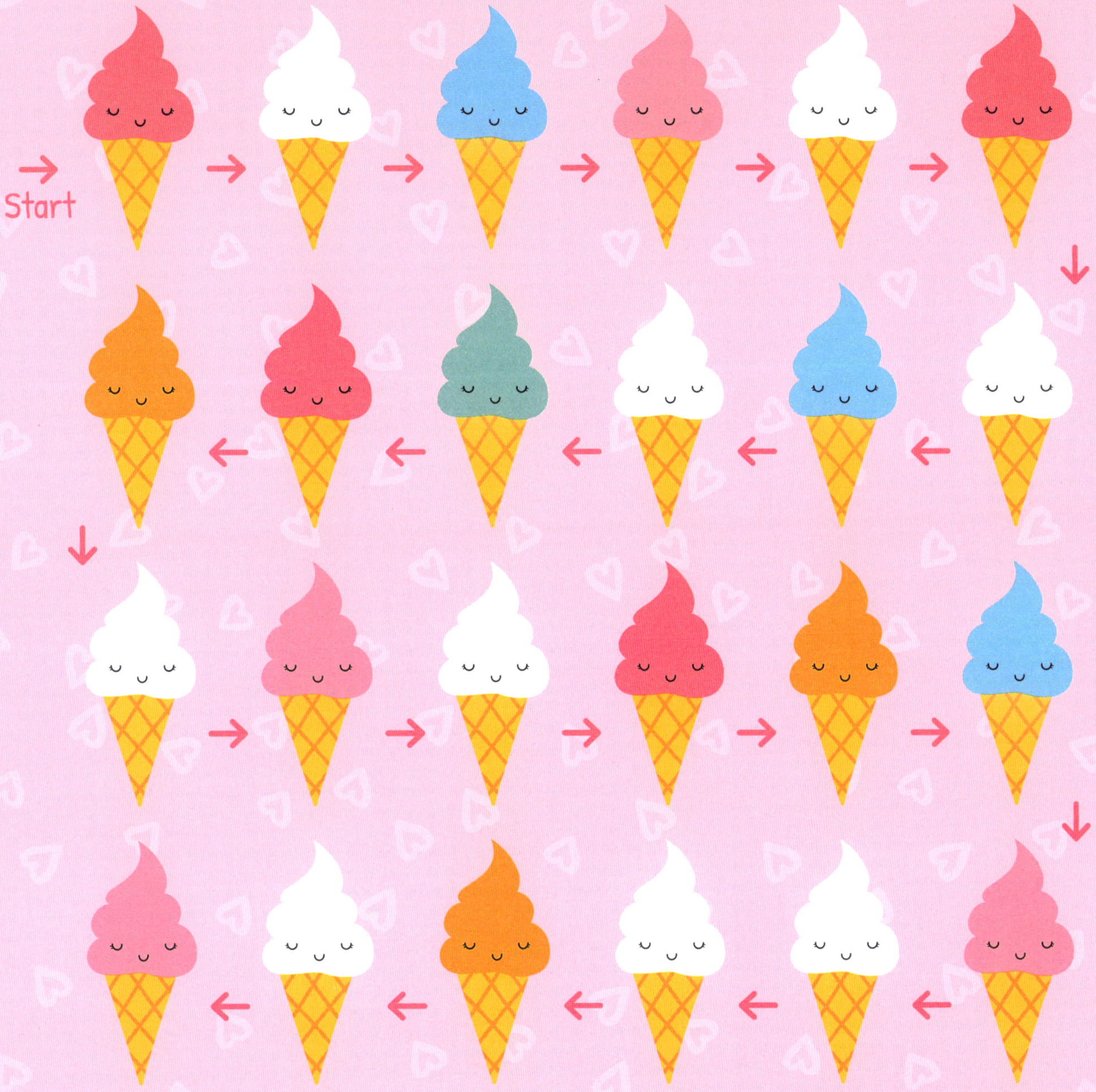

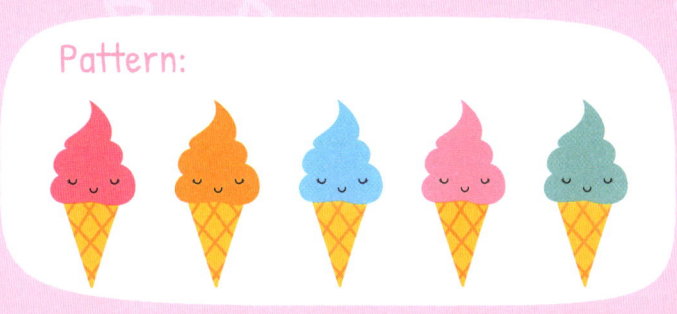

Pattern:

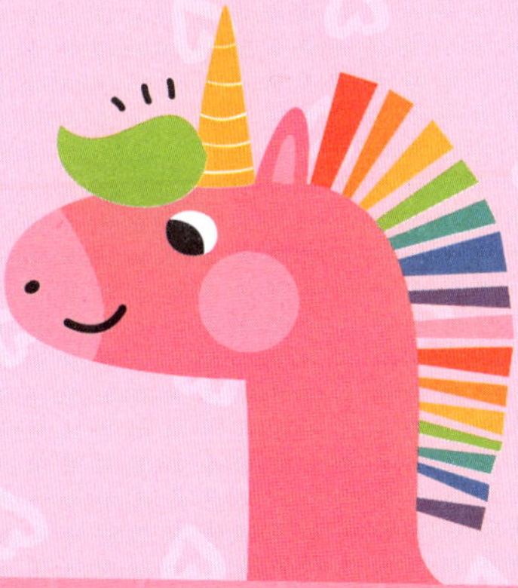

COMPLETE THE PATTERN

Complete the pattern by coloring in the ice-cream cones and following the arrows!

WHERE IS MY SHADOW?
Which shadow belongs to Zelda?

A	U	D	W	S	K	Y	C	H	P
S	I	N	R	I	R	E	R	O	A
T	C	M	I	E	N	E	O	O	G
A	O	R	A	C	A	G	W	V	L
R	U	M	A	N	O	M	N	E	I
T	R	R	O	S	E	R	S	S	T
D	I	A	M	O	N	D	N	T	T
I	H	O	R	N	N	E	S	E	E
L	N	M	A	G	I	C	U	E	R
R	A	I	N	B	O	W	G	E	S

UNICORN - MANE - HOOVES - GLITTER - DREAMS
CROWN - SKY - WING - STAR - MAGIC
DIAMOND - ROSE - RAINBOW - MOON - HORN

WORD SEARCH
Circle the unicorn terms in the grid.
They can be written side to side,
up and down, or diagonally.

33

SEEK AND FIND
Look through all the fluttering creatures to find and circle these drawings within!

Rules of the Game

1

Take turns with another player. Player 1 draws a circle in the grid wherever they want.

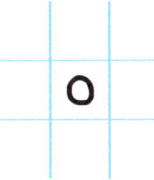

2

Player 2 draws an X in another box, wherever they want.

3

The first player to align three of their symbols up and down, side to side, or diagonally wins!

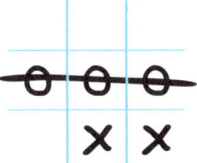

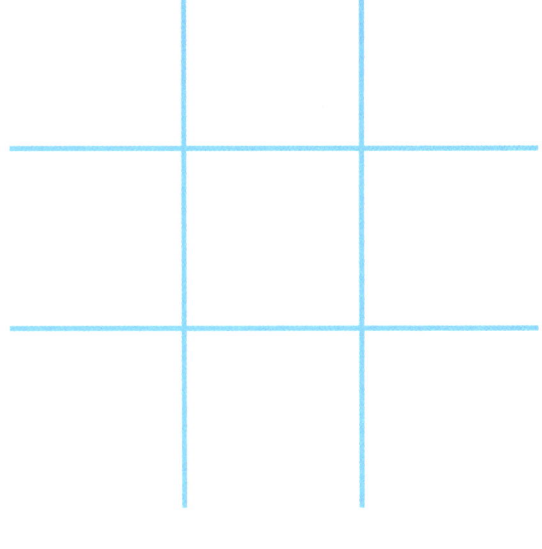

Two Players

TIC-TAC-TOE

Match three of the same symbols in a row up and down, side to side, or diagonally to win! Fill this page and the next with your matches.

35

36

SUDOKU
Complete the grid so that the numbers one to four are found on each line, in each column, and in each group of four boxes.

FIND THE PATH
Which path should Coco take to reach the rainbow?

CODED MESSAGE
Fill in the circles with the letters that appear under the symbol in the key up top. Use this method to decode Bubblegum's message!

SUDO-COLORS
Color the hearts in blue, green, pink, yellow, orange, or red. Each color must appear only once on each row, in each column, and in each group of six boxes.

MASK

Cut out the unicorn mask, including the eyes, and use a hole punch to make holes on the sides (where the gray dots are). Tie a ribbon from one hole to the other and adjust the mask to fit your head size!

Color your mask. You can wear it on this side or the other; you choose!

MAZE

Sprinkles danced with the stars all night long.
She needs to find the right path to get to her cloud for some rest.
Show her the way!

HAVE YOU SEEN SKY DANCER?
Out of all the unicorns on the page,
find this one and circle him.

PORTRAIT
Only one of these portraits of Lemon Drop the llamacorn is correct. Which one is it?

ODD ONE OUT
Cherry Blossom loves to fly in outer space.
Find which object doesn't belong and circle it!

TREASURE BOX

Cut out the box and fold it along the dotted lines.
Put glue on tab 1, then glue the bottom of the box shut.
Put glue on tab 2, then glue the side of the box shut.

You can choose to color your box before assembling it.
Then, glue it so that your drawing is on the outside!

MAZE
Blueberry got lost in the snow!
Help her find the way to the rainbow.

ODD ONE OUT
Unicorns love to fly among the butterflies.
Find the object that doesn't belong and circle it!

SOLVE THE RIDDLE
Solve the riddle to find out which of these llamacorns brought Juniper a cupcake!

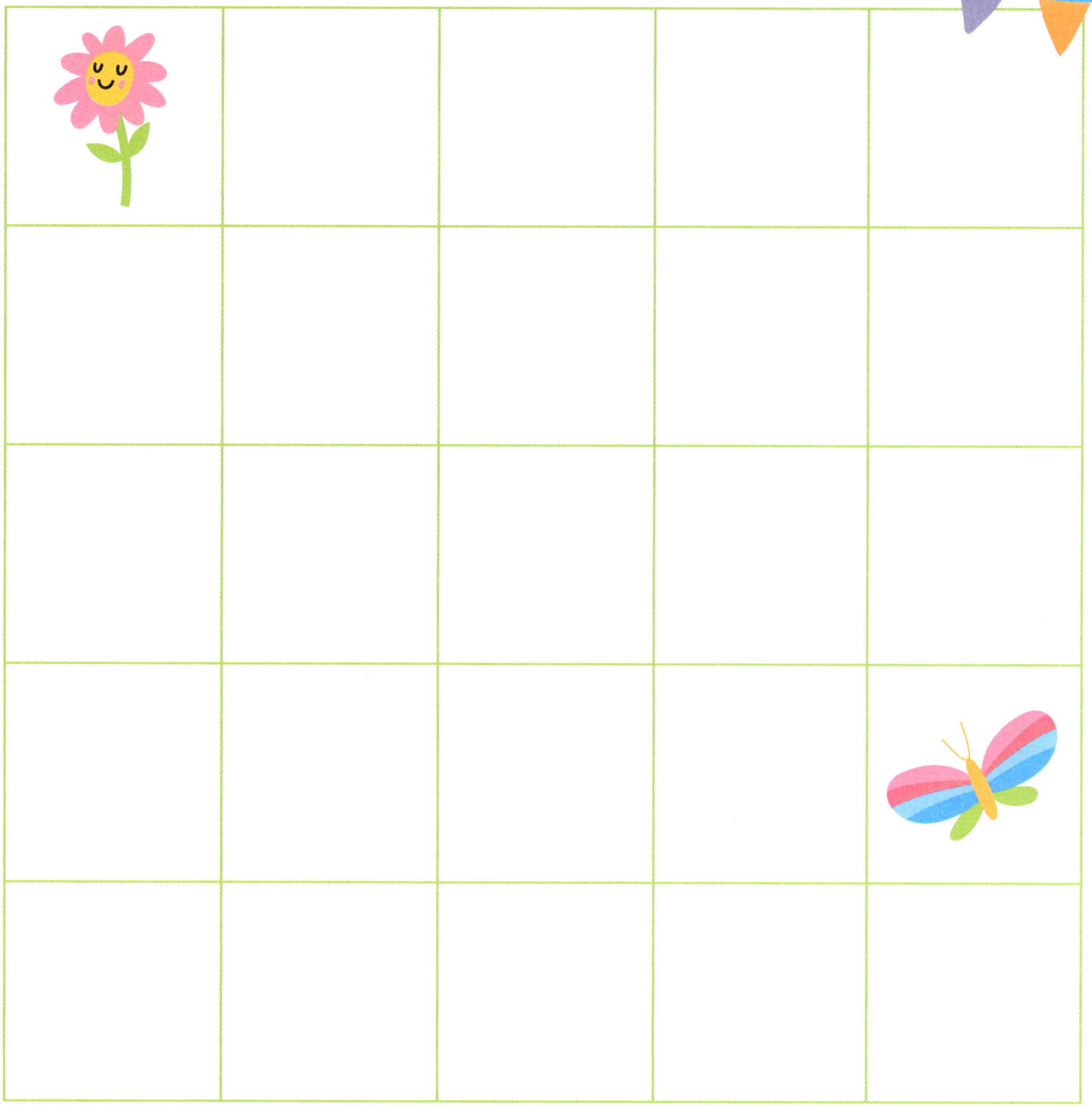

1: ↑ ← ↓ ↓ ← ← ↑ ← ↓
2: ↑ ← ↓ ← ↑ ↑ ← ← ↑
3: ← ← ↑ ← ← ↓ ↓ → →

CODING
The butterfly needs to find its flower, but it doesn't have the correct code! Which of these three codes is the correct one if you start in the box with the butterfly?

SPOT THE DIFFERENCES
Find and circle the seven differences between these two images!

54

HAVE YOU SEEN THIS GIFT?
Rainbow is invited to a birthday party.
Help her find this gift by circling it!

SOLVE THE RIDDLE
Solve the riddle and find out which of these castles belongs to Amethyst!

MAZE
Honeydew wants to find her friend. Which path should she take?

L	S	C	O	R	A	L	T
V	A	K	G	R	E	E	N
O	I	V	Y	M	I	N	T
R	B	O	E	B	O	S	E
A	R	P	L	N	L	A	A
N	O	I	L	E	D	U	L
G	W	N	O	Q	T	E	E
E	N	K	W	R	E	D	R

ORANGE – YELLOW – VIOLET – TEAL
PINK – BROWN – MINT – CORAL – RED
SKY BLUE – GREEN – LAVENDER

WORD SEARCH

Circle the names of colors in the grid.
They can be written side to side, up and down, or diagonally.

TWO BY TWO
The unicorns are all mixed up!
Connect them to make pairs.

SPOT THE DIFFERENCES
Find and circle the seven differences between these two images!

FIND THE PATH

Topaz wants to bring her friend two pink cupcakes and four blue cupcakes.
Which path should she take?

SOLVE THE RIDDLE
Solve the riddle to find out which of these owls is Meadow's best friend!

HOW FAST CAN YOU COUNT?
How many of each object is on the page?
Write the answers in the bubbles.

PUZZLE

Match the last three pieces to complete the puzzle!
Put the correct number in each blank cloud shape.

TWO BY TWO
The unicorns are all mixed up!
Connect them to make pairs.

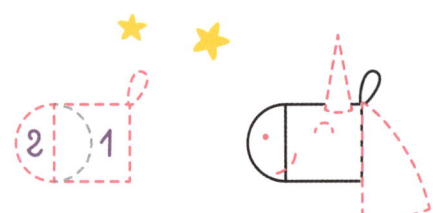
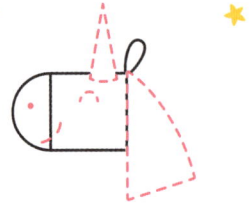

1. Draw a square. Draw a loop on the upper right corner.

2. Draw a circle so that the center is the left side of the square.

3. Draw a horn on top of the square, then a mane, eyes, smile, and nostril.

4. Draw a larger circle for the body, and a football shape for the tail. Underneath, draw four skinny rectangles for the legs.

5. Color it all in!

DRAW THE UNICORN
Learn to draw a unicorn, color it, then fill the page with unicorn friends!

SPOT THE DIFFERENCES
Find and circle the seven differences between these two images.

```
D B W B E L R E C S
E L E O I R E U S Q
E P O A L R N U A U
R L I U R F D N O I
S R A C C O O N W R
S N A I L X D F L R
O P E S K U N K I E
N L O T T E R N E L
R A B B I T N D R E
E M F R O G A N P S
```

SQUIRREL – OWL – SNAIL
BEAR – WOLF – RABBIT
BIRD – RACCOON – OTTER
FROG – FOX – DEER – SKUNK

WORD SEARCH

Circle the forest creatures in the grid.
They can be written side to side, up and down, or diagonally.

68

Rules of the Game

1. You and a friend will use your own special colors to draw lines between two dots.
2. One friend draws lines side to side, and the other friend draws lines up and down. Each dot can only have one line.
3. The game ends when one person can't draw any more lines. The friend who draws the last line wins!

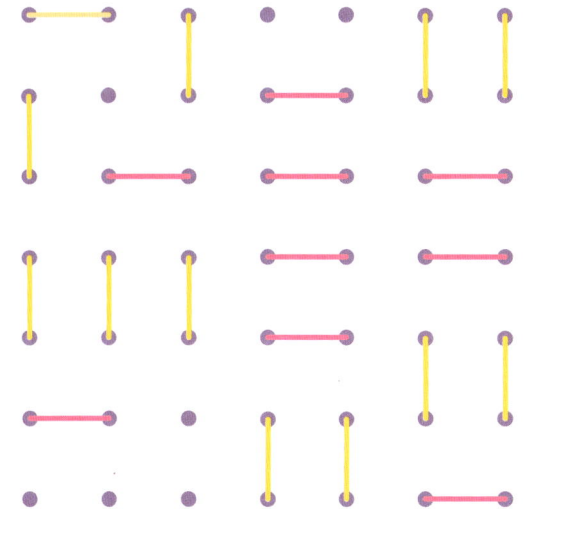

Two Players

CONNECT THE DOTS

This is a fun game for two friends to play together. Use two different colored pencils to draw lines on the paper. When you finish both rounds, you can use the next page to keep the fun going!

HOW FAST CAN YOU COUNT?
How many of each flower is on the page?
Write the answers in the bubbles.

TWO BY TWO
The hot-air balloons are all mixed up!
Connect them to make pairs.

1

2

3

4

5

PORTRAIT
Only one of these portraits of Rainbow is correct.
Which one is it?

ODD ONE OUT
An object is hidden among the flowers.
Find where it is and circle it!

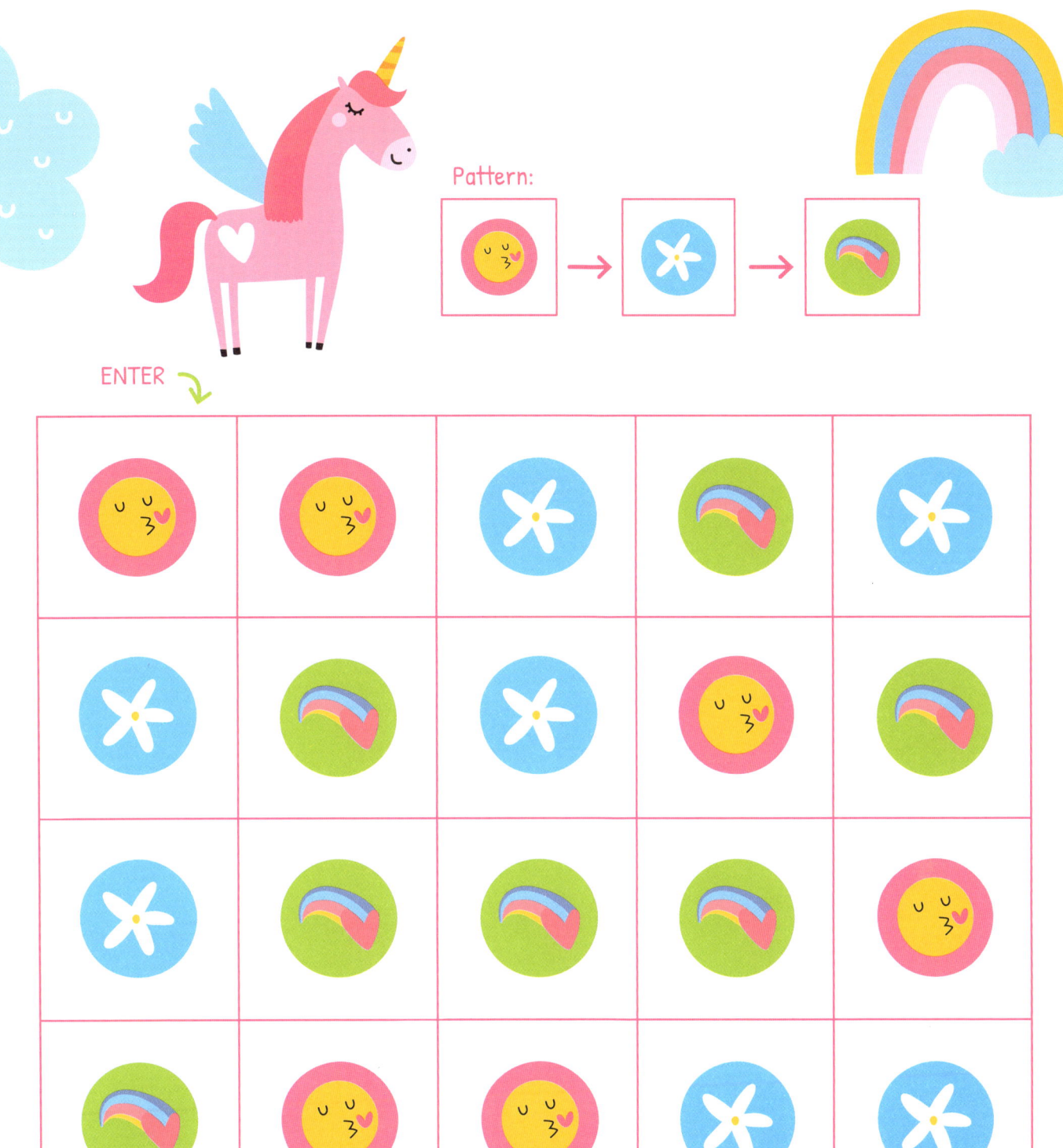

FOLLOW THE PATTERN
Help Aurora find the exit by following the pattern of symbols.
It can move side to side or up and down.

PUZZLE
Match the last three pieces to complete the puzzle!
Put the correct number in each blank circle.

SEEK AND FIND
Look throughout the scene to find and circle these objects within!

TWO BY TWO
The unicorns are all mixed up!
Connect them to make pairs.

HOW FAST CAN YOU COUNT?
How many of these strawberries are there on the page?
Write the answer in the bubble.

1: ← ↑ → ↓ → ↑ ↑

2: ↓ → ↑ ↑ ↑ →

3: ↓ ↓ → → ↑ ← ↑

CODING

Princess Raspberry needs to find her crown, but she has to avoid the arrows. Which of these three codes is the correct one if you start in the box with the unicorn?

WHERE IS MY SHADOW?
Match each flower to its shadow.

J	N	E	P	T	U	N	E
S	U	R	A	N	U	S	A
A	M	P	L	U	T	O	R
T	A	A	I	P	L	T	T
U	N	E	R	T	T	E	H
R	N	A	I	S	E	R	N
N	M	E	R	C	U	R	Y
E	V	E	N	U	S	E	E

EARTH – SATURN – JUPITER
MERCURY – VENUS – PLUTO – NEPTUNE
URANUS – MARS

WORD SEARCH
Circle the names of planets in the grid.
They can be written side to side, up and down, or diagonally.

- Her horn is the color of the rainbow
- She has no ribbon in her mane
- Her nose is blue
- She has stars on her back

SOLVE THE RIDDLE
Solve the riddle to find out which unicorn's castle sits among the clouds!

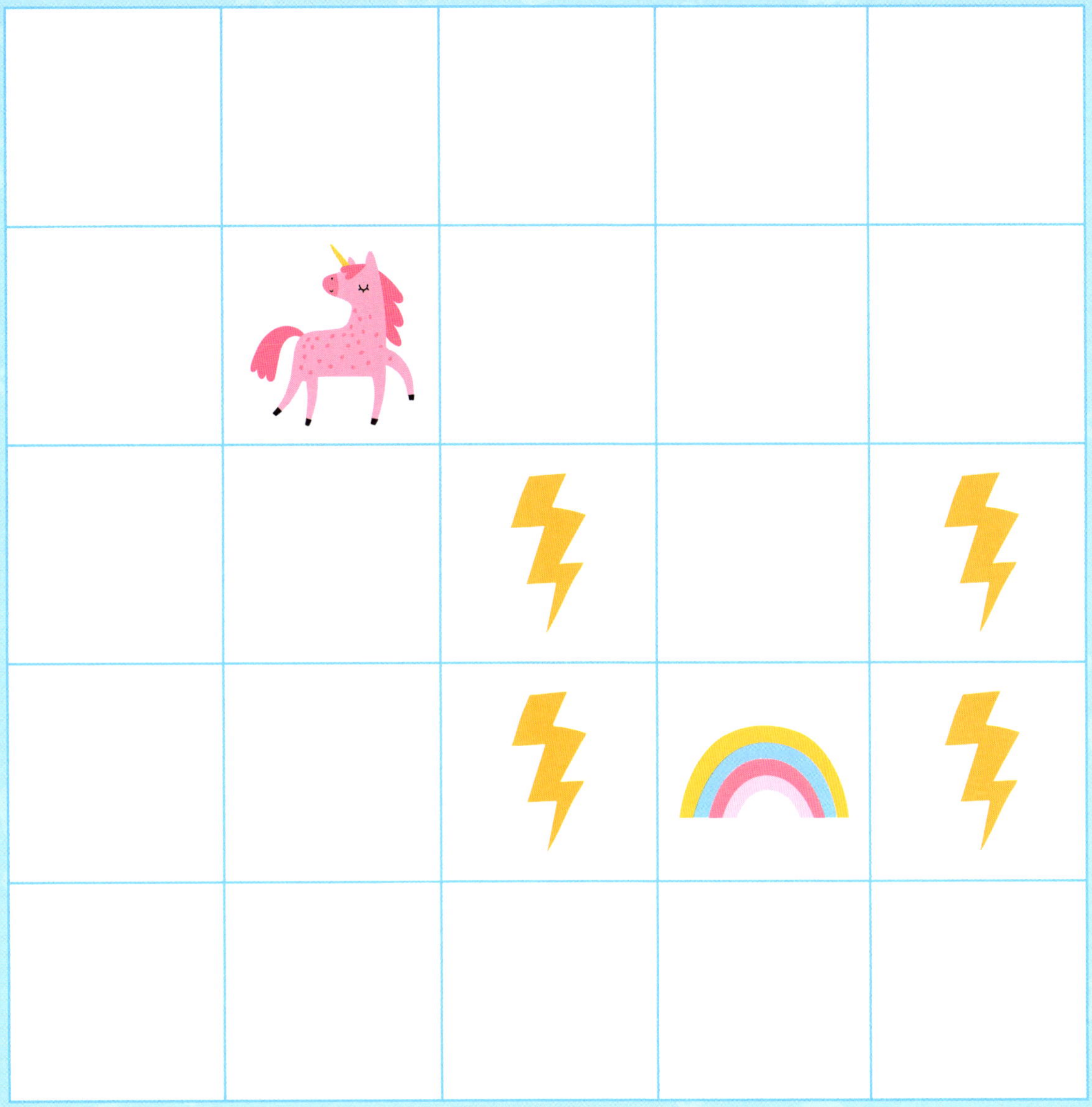

1: ↓ ↓ → ↑ ↑ → →

2: → ↑ → → ↓ ↓ ↓

3: → ↑ → ↓ ↓ ↓

CODING

Mystic needs to reach the rainbow, but she has to avoid the lightning strikes. Which of these three codes is the correct one if you start in the box with the unicorn?

PUZZLE
Match the last three pieces to complete the puzzle!
Put the correct number in each blank circle.

SEEK AND FIND
Look throughout the scene to find and circle these rainbows within!

FIND THE PATH
Zelda must find her friends in the forest.
Which path should she take to bring them five pine cones?

Pattern:

COMPLETE THE PATTERN
Complete the pattern by coloring in the clouds and following the arrows!

SOLUTIONS

P. 3 :

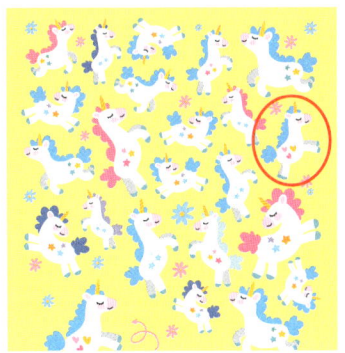

P. 4 : 1

P. 5 :

S	D	C	U	L	O
L	U	O	D	S	C
O	C	S	L	U	D
C	L	D	S	O	U
U	O	L	C	D	S
D	S	U	O	C	L

P. 6 :

P. 9 :

P. 10 :

P. 11 :

5	1	6	3	2	4
3	4	2	6	5	1
6	2	5	4	1	3
4	3	1	5	6	2
2	6	4	1	3	5
1	5	3	2	4	6

P. 12 : 3

P. 13 :

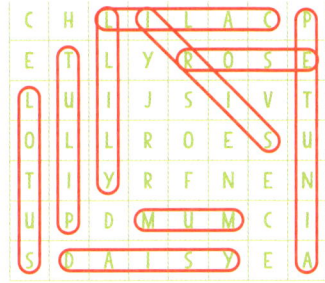

P. 14 :

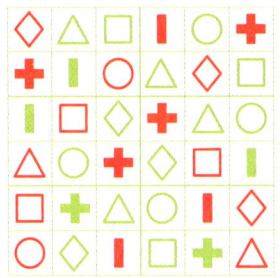

P. 16 :

R	E	S	O
O	S	E	R
S	R	O	E
E	O	R	S

P. 17 :

P. 18 :

P. 19 :

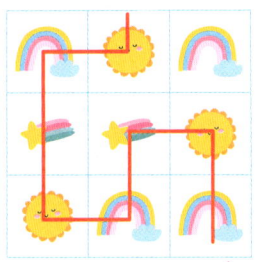

P. 20 :

P. 21 :

P. 22 :

93

SOLUTIONS

P. 23 : 2

P. 24 : 5

P. 25 :

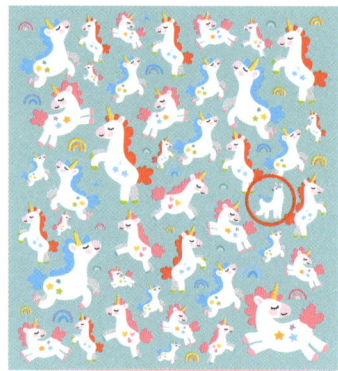

P. 26 : 3

P. 27 :

P. 29 : 2

P. 30 : 3

P. 31 :

P. 32 : 3

P. 33 :

P. 34 :

P. 37 :

P. 38 :

P. 39 : Chase your dreams

P. 40 :

P. 43 :

P. 44 :

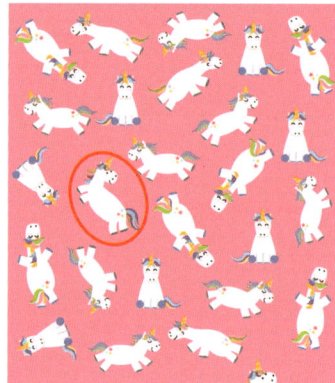

P. 45 : 3

P. 46 :

SOLUTIONS

P. 49 :

P. 50 :

P. 52 : 4

P. 53 : 2

P. 54 :

P. 55 :

P. 56 : 2

P. 57 :

P. 58 :

P. 59 :

P. 60 :

P. 61 :

P. 62 : 3

P. 63 :

P. 64 :

P. 65 :

P. 67 :

P. 68 :

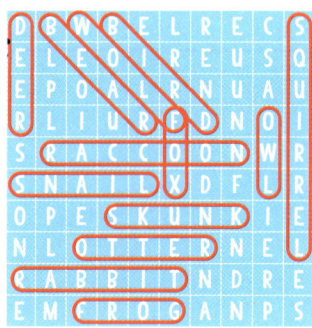

P. 71 :

SOLUTIONS

P. 72 :

P. 73 : 2

P. 74 :

P. 75 :

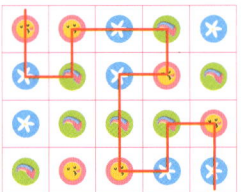

P. 76 :

P. 77 :

P. 79 :

P. 80 : 13

P. 81 : 2

P. 82 :

P. 84 :

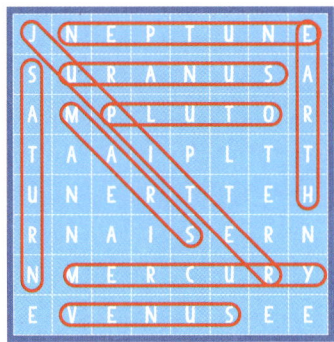

P. 86 : 1

P. 87 : 3

P. 88 :

P. 89 :

P. 90 :

P. 91 :